for Mum and Dad, with love and gratitude,
and for my ever-creative muse
PB

for Mini Minnie and
Minnie's mum and dad
GP-R

LITTLE TIGER PRESS
An imprint of Magi Publications
1 The Coda Centre, 189 Munster Road, London SW6 6AW
www.littletigerpress.com

First published in Great Britain 2003
This edition published 2005

ISBN-13: 978-1-84506-238-5 · ISBN-10: 1-84506-238-8
Printed in China
6 8 10 9 7 5

Paul Bright   Guy Parker-Rees

LITTLE TIGER PRESS
London

Deep, deep in the jungle,
chimps were chattering,

frogs were croaking,

birds were screeching,

and a million insects were
humming and buzzing.
What a lot of noise!

It was time for
baby Leo to have his morning nap.
"He'll never get to sleep with all this din,"
said Ma Lion. "Isn't there something
you can do?"

"Do?" said Pa Lion. "Do?
I am king of the beasts. Of course
there is something I can do!"
He stood up tall, puffed out his
huge chest, and roared . . .

And baby Leo slept. Pa Lion
whispered softly, but so clearly that all
of the creatures could hear him:

"And if any of you makes a noise,
and wakes up Leo, I will eat you."

All was quiet in the jungle.
Quiet as the morning mist.
Quiet as the opening flowers.
Quiet as a baby sleeping.
Suddenly . . .

Cawing and crowing, squeaking and squawking.
Beaks pecking and claws scratching.
Two parrots were arguing in the bushes!

"**Quiet!**" said Pa Lion, as loud as he dared.
"It's all right," said Ma Lion. "Leo's still fast asleep."
"I can't eat the parrots, then," said Pa Lion sulkily.
"No, my dear," said Ma Lion, "you can't eat the parrots."
"Bother," said Pa Lion. "I could do with a snack."

All was quiet in the jungle.
Quiet as the trees growing towards the sky.
Quiet as the leaves reaching towards the light.
Quiet as a baby sleeping.
Suddenly . . .

Chuckling
and chortling,

sniggering
and snickering.

The hyena was laughing.
Laughing like hyenas do.

But nobody knew what was so funny.

"Quiet!" said Pa Lion, as loud as he dared.
"It's all right," said Ma Lion. "Leo's still asleep."
"I can't eat the hyena, then," said Pa Lion crossly.
"No, my dear," said Ma Lion. "You can't eat the hyena."
"Bother!" said Pa Lion.
"I'm beginning to feel quite peckish."

All was quiet in the jungle.
Quiet as the calm after a storm.
Quiet as sunshine after rain.
Quiet as a baby sleeping.
Suddenly . . .

Howling and hooting, screeching and chattering. Swinging and swooping. A family of monkeys was leaping through the trees!

"**Quiet!**" said Pa Lion, as loud as he dared.
"It's all right," said Ma Lion. "Leo's still asleep."
"I can't eat the monkeys, then," said Pa Lion grumpily.
"No, my dear," said Ma Lion. "You can't eat the monkeys."
"Bother!" said Pa Lion. "I'm hungry now, really hungry."

It was the middle of the day
and the jungle was hot and humid.
The animals sheltered in the shade of the
trees, drowsy and dozing.

All was quiet in the jungle.
Quiet as the blazing sun.
Quiet as the shadows underneath the trees.
Quiet as a baby sleeping.
Suddenly . . .

Splashing and squelching.

Ooohing and aaahing.

A hippopotamus was
yawning in the cool muddy
shallows of the river.

"**Quiet!**" said Pa Lion, as loud as he dared.

"It's all right," said Ma Lion. "Leo's still fast asleep."

"I can't eat the hippopotamus, then," said Pa Lion despairingly.

"Sometimes, my dear," said Ma Lion, "your eyes
are bigger than your belly. No,
you can't eat the hippopotamus."

"Bother," said Pa Lion.

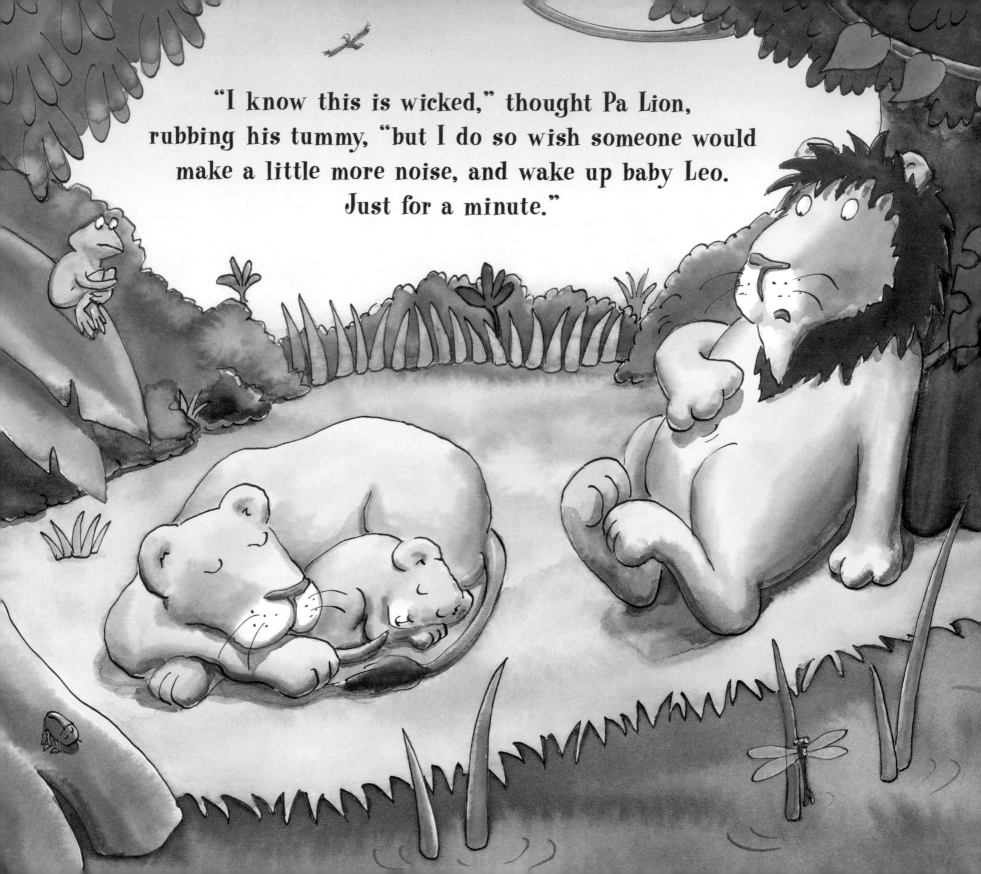

"I know this is wicked," thought Pa Lion,
rubbing his tummy, "but I do so wish someone would
make a little more noise, and wake up baby Leo.
Just for a minute."

But all was quiet in the jungle.
Quiet as a fish swimming in the river.
Quiet as a bird soaring in the sky.
Quiet as a baby sleeping.
Suddenly . . .

A rumbling and grumbling,
a groaning and moaning, a gurgling and burbling.
A noise like nothing ever heard before.

Loud as thunder.
Loud as banging drums.
Loud as a baby crying!

"Who has woken baby Leo?" cried Ma Lion.
"Find who it is, Pa. Find them and eat them!"

Now!

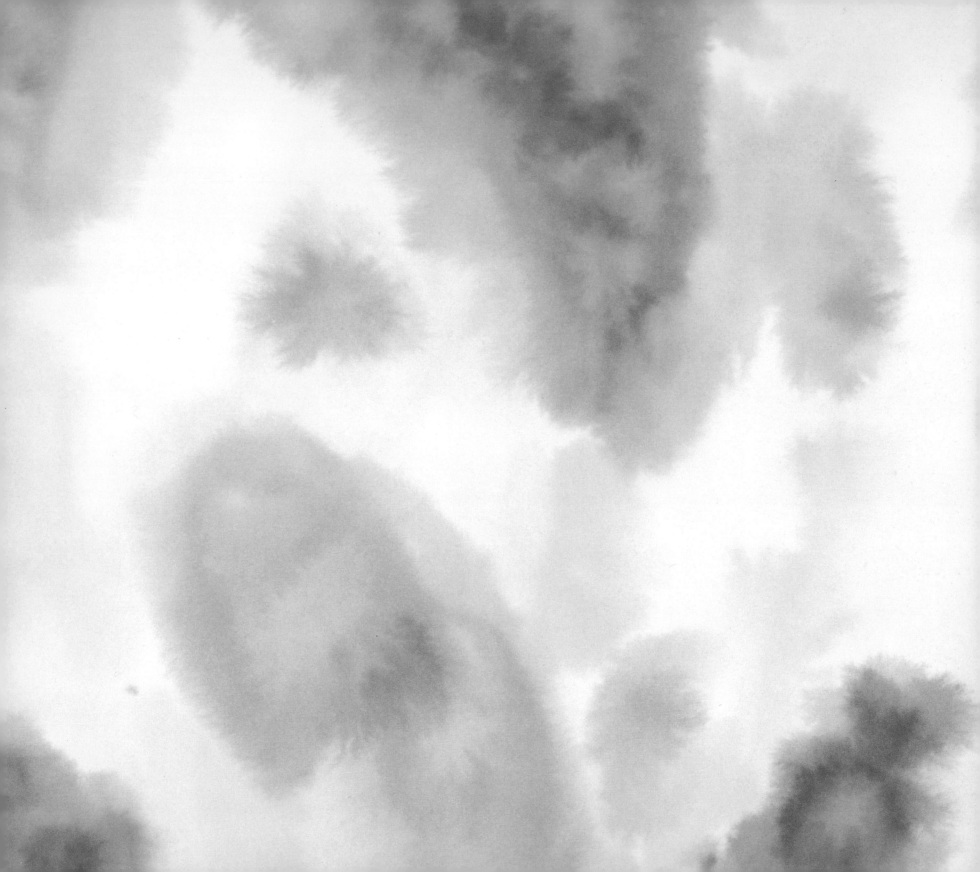

Roaring good reads from Little Tiger Press

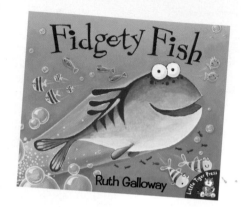

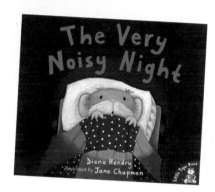

For information regarding
any of the above titles or for
our catalogue, please contact us:
Little Tiger Press, 1 The Coda Centre,
189 Munster Road, London SW6 6AW, UK
Tel: 020 7385 6333 Fax: 020 7385 7333
E-mail: info@littletiger.co.uk
www.littletigerpress.com